USBORNE

Penny Dreadful

is a Magnet for Disaster

3 stories in one book!

Joanna Nadin

"Do not even think about it, Penelope Jones."
Aunt Deedee

"Did I ever tell you I could have been a
ballet dancer if I hadn't met your mother?"
Dad

"I have my beady eye on you."
Mrs. Butterworth

"Heavens to Betsy!"
Gran

"Penelope Jones, I am completely **DISCOMBOBULATED**
as to why you have spelled 'Orangutan' with a Q."
Miss Patterson

"Meow..."
Barry

Penny Dreadful

is a Magnet for Disaster

By Joanna Nadin

Illustrated by Jess Mikhail

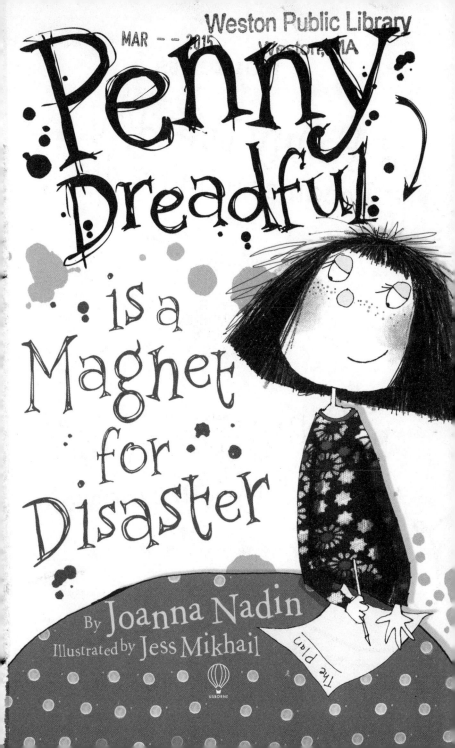

USBORNE

Contents

Penny Dreadful
and the School Inspector
page 95

Penny Dreadful's
Top 5 Tips for Survival
page 134

Meet **Penny Dreadful** and her Resigned Relations

Penny
(It's never really her fault…)

Cosmo
(Penny's best friend)

Georgia May Morton-Jones
(Penny's genius cousin)

Daisy
(Penny's annoying sister)

Penny's
long-suffering **mom** and **dad**

Very prim-and-proper
Aunt Deedee

Barry
(Meow, I'm Gran's cat)

Gran
(Normally found fast asleep somewhere)

Penny Dreadful

Becomes a Hairstylist

My name is not actually Penny Dreadful.

It is Penelope Jones. The "Dreadful" part is my dad's **JOKE**. I know it is a joke because every time he says it he laughs like a honking goose. But I do not see the funny side. Plus it is not even true that I am dreadful. It is like Gran says, i.e. that I am a **MAGNET FOR DISASTER**. Mom says if Gran kept a better eye on me in the first place instead of on Chuck Hernandez, soap opera superstar, then I might not be quite so magnetic. But Gran says if Mom wasn't so busy answering phones for Dr. Cement, who is her boss and who has bulgy eyes like hard-boiled eggs (which is why everyone calls him Dr. Bugeye), and Dad wasn't so busy solving crises at the city council, then they would be able to solve some crises at 73 Rollins Road, i.e. our house. So you see it is completely not my fault.

★ ☆ ★ ✦

Anyway when I get up this morning I am full of gloom even though it is the weekend because of several things, i.e.:

1. My sister Daisy, who is eleven, and very irritating, is doubly irritating because she is going to Monkey Madness safari park tomorrow and is pleased as punch.

b. I am not allowed to go to Monkey Madness safari park because Mom says there is too much **POTENTIAL FOR CATASTROPHE**, plus it costs $15 and I still owe her $10.75 for the time I accidentally called India.

3. There are no Sugar Pops left for breakfast because Gran's cat Barry has eaten the last bowlful, even though Mom has told Gran that Barry is supposed to eat **CAT FOOD AND CAT FOOD ONLY**.

But then it gets completely
worse because the doorbell rings
and it is Aunt Deedee, who is
dropping off Georgia May
Morton-Jones, i.e. my cousin,
because she has a **CRUCIAL
MEETING WITH THE NEW
YORK OFFICE** and has fired
Katya Romanov (who is the
nanny) for **NOT
MEASURING UP**. Aunt
Deedee is Dad's sister,
although Gran says
sometimes she thinks she
brought the wrong baby
back from the hospital

because she is not at all like Dad, i.e. she does not ever wear wrinkled slacks or drink orange juice from the carton (which Mom says is unhygienic but everyone does it, even Daisy). Plus Aunt Deedee is always firing nannies for **NOT MEASURING UP**. Although Gran says not even the Queen of Sheba would **MEASURE UP** in Aunt Deedee's eyes.

Anyway Mom says she is working all day because Dr. Cement has a bunion clinic and Dad is at the council solving a crisis to do with some parking meters so Gran is in charge. Then Aunt Deedee's eyes start to squint because she is not big on Gran being in charge ever since the time she let Georgia May Morton-Jones eat mud because she said it would give her the

CONSTITUTION OF AN OX, but as Gran says

BEGGARS CAN'T BE CHOOSERS so Aunt

Deedee says,

Fine, but there is to be absolutely no messy play, no eating dirt and, Penelope Jones, if you even think of persuading Georgia May Morton-Jones to run away to the North Pole again I will quite possibly spontaneously combust.

I say I am too gloomy to run away, even though seeing Aunt Deedee spontaneously combust would be quite interesting. Aunt Deedee says "Good" and then goes back to shouting into her phone at someone named Henrietta.

But now I am even more gloomy because Georgia May Morton-Jones is here all day and she is only four and a half and not usually interested in any of my **BRILLIANT IDEAS™** in case she ruins her clothes or her fingers, which are very important because Mr. Nakamura says she shows potential on the violin. I do not show potential on the violin, although I did do "Twinkle Twinkle Little Star" on the recorder at the Fall Festival last year and I only got five notes wrong.

13

So what happens is we have to play cards all morning until Gran makes us corned beef sandwiches for lunch, only Georgia May has cheese because she says the corned beef looks like cat food and she is not allowed cat food after last time. And I am just thinking that I might die of boredom when the doorbell rings again. Gran says "It is like Piccadilly Circus around here," which Daisy says is not actually a circus with lions and a trapeze at all, it is just a road with a lot of cars so Gran is wrong on all counts. But this time it is Cosmo

Webster, i.e. my best friend (even though he is a boy and exactly a week older, because neither of those things are his fault), and amazingly he has **NO HAIR**. Gran says,

Heavens to Betsy, Cosmo, what happened to you?

Because normally Cosmo has hair that is even longer than mine.

Cosmo says, "*It is because of the lice.*"
What has happened is that Cosmo's
mother, who is called Sunflower even
though her real name is Barbara,
does not believe in chemicals or
killing innocent insects, so she has
tried to persuade the lice to leave
by using a special chant. But the
lice have not been listening and
instead they multiplied like **CRAZY** and Cosmo's
head was very itchy, so Sunflower said he had to
get it cut, but she could not do it because **a)**
her scissors are lost from when we used them as
divining rods to find water under the merry-
go-round, and **2.** hair is a sign of strength and
she cannot be the one to **SAP HIS POWERS**.

16

So he has been to
Hair Today and
Shaniqua Reynolds has
cut it all off for $15.

And that is when
I have the first

BRILLIANT IDEA™

which is **TO BECOME A HAIRSTYLIST**, because
I have figured out I only need to do one and a
half haircuts to pay Mom back for calling
India and then I will be able to go to Monkey
Madness safari park with Daisy.
And Aunt Deedee did not say
NO HAIRSTYLING so it is fine.

So then me and Cosmo go into my office, i.e. my bedroom, and write a list of all the people we can give haircuts to and Georgia May comes too because Gran wants to watch *Animal SOS*, which is a TV series where animals are always almost dying but then they don't and it is **MIRACULOUS**, and Georgia May is not allowed to watch TV unless it is the Math Channel. By the time we have finished we have five people on our list, i.e.:

1. Gran

b. Barry. Even though he is a cat we will still charge $15 because he is very hairy and the part on his bottom is tangled from when he sat on a piece of Cosmo's bubblegum.

3. Daisy

4. Bridget Grimes, who is in our class and has very long hair that actually reaches her waist and she is always swishing it and saying "My hair actually reaches my waist, Penelope Jones," but Mom says it needs a good cut.

e. Brady O'Grady, who is also in our class but he has his head shaved every week, sometimes with patterns in it, so it will be an easy job.

And Cosmo has made a notice out of the back of my Dogs of the World poster and a glitter pen and it says **GET YOUR HARE CUT HERE**, which looks really **EYE-CATCHING** even though Georgia May points out it is the wrong kind of hare, but I say the first rule of business is being **EYE-CATCHING** not spelling correctly, so we put the poster up on my door and wait.

And then what happens
is that Daisy comes out
of her bedroom with
Lucy B. Finnegan
(who once got
her finger stuck
in the drain in
our bathroom sink)
to see what all the **FUSS**
is about, and Daisy says, "Penelope Jones,
you are a **MORON** if you think anyone
will let you cut their hair."

And Lucy B. Finnegan says, "You've
spelled 'hair' wrong, too." And then they
are killing themselves laughing, so we decide to
go to the store to do our haircuts because it is

too distracting with all
the noise at home.
But when we
get to the store I
realize I have
totally not got
any scissors because
they are in the
kitchen in the **OFF**

LIMITS drawer after I used them to cut up an
old curtain for an emergency rope ladder (only it
wasn't an *old* curtain at all), and so I am like a
wizard without a wand. Cosmo says we need to
borrow some from somebody and I say maybe
we can ask Mrs. Butterworth at the general store
because even though she is always saying stuff

like "I have got my beady eye on you," she also has a mustache, so I think we can offer to cut it in exchange for the scissors and our collateral, which means our money, which is a dollar bill that Cosmo found in his pocket.

★ ☆ ✦ ✷

The general store sign says

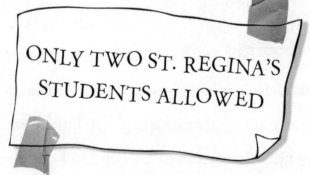

ONLY TWO ST. REGINA'S STUDENTS ALLOWED

but it is okay because Georgia May is not at St. Regina's, she is at The Greely Academy for Girls, so when we go in Mrs. Butterworth cannot say a thing except for,

And I say, "No but my gran does," which is almost true because only just a minute ago I said, "Goodbye, Gran, we are going to the store to cut hair for money." And she said, "Super." Although I am not sure if it was to me or because a hamster had just not died **MIRACULOUSLY** on the television, but I did not decide to find out, so off we went.

Mrs. Butterworth does not ask if Cosmo's mother knows where he is because Cosmo's mother is always saying how she believes in **FREEDOM** and **SELF-EXPRESSION**, i.e. Cosmo is allowed to do what he likes so he can learn to be **RESPONSIBLE**, etc. You can tell Mrs. Butterworth does not believe in **FREEDOM** or **SELF-EXPRESSION**, but she does believe in haircuts because what she does say is, "It *is* about time you had your hair cut — it was hard to tell if you were a boy or a girl, Cosmo Moon Webster." Cosmo says "I have other evidence" but Mrs. Butterworth does not want to see the other evidence. Nor does she want to lend us scissors in exchange for cutting her mustache, which she says is not a mustache at all and she will be reporting me to my mother for saying it is.

So then we do not have any scissors and I am already in trouble and we have spent our collateral on licorice sticks and are chewing them on the wall outside, when we see Bridget Grimes riding her bike

down the sidewalk. She says,

What are you doing loitering, Penelope Jones?

And I say, "We are not loitering we are
giving haircuts, only we don't have any
scissors — can we borrow some and
cut your hair, it is only $15?" She says,
"Absolutely not and I would not do
that if I were you, Penelope Jones."

Which is what she is always saying because she is the star student in our class and our principal Mr. Schumann's favorite. But luckily Georgia May Morton-Jones says, "You shouldn't be riding on the sidewalk, Bridget Grimes, it is against the law and you will be arrested and put in prison." And Bridget Grimes shuts up, and I am glad that Georgia May Morton-Jones came after all because sometimes knowing a lot of rules is useful.

But we still don't have any scissors and then Cosmo sees Brady O'Grady coming out of the butcher's shop with Mrs. O'Grady (who has a tattoo of a heart and a dagger on her arm) and it is **OBVIOUS** that he has quite recently had all his hair shaved off, even the cross which was

there before, and so he won't need it done again
for at least three days. But this gives me another

BRILLIANT IDEA™,

which is that, even though we do not have
scissors, Dad has an electric razor and I am not
even banned from using it yet. So we go all the
way back home again.

✦ ✦ ✦ ✦

The razor is amazing. It is called the Silent
Trimmer and has three lengths and two speeds,
i.e. *fast* and *super fast*. On the ad it says **THE
CLOSEST SHAVE** and I know it is true because
Aunt Deedee wrote the ad. Cosmo says, "Have
you ever used it before?" And I say, "No but
I have watched Dad about a gazillion

times and it cannot be that hard because Dad is not good with machines, e.g. the DVD player which he still does not know how to use after two years." But Cosmo says we should test it first so we decide to try

Barry because he can't complain and also he is very hairy. Cosmo says he will be in charge of the Trimmer because he is a week older and also a boy and boys are better at machines, but I remind him about **a)** Dad and the DVD player,

b) that Sunflower is always getting on to him for saying stuff like that, and **3)** that it is more my razor than his so I will do it.

But I am soon regretting it because when I shave the top of Barry's head he scratches me on the nose and I am mortally wounded.

Cosmo says it would not have happened if he was in charge and that I am too injured to go on, but I say it is fine, I am like *Animal SOS* and will **MIRACULOUSLY NOT DIE**. But I decide that I have trimmed enough of Barry (plus he has hidden himself inside the dishwasher and I am not allowed to touch the dishwasher for a lot of reasons) so we should trim Gran instead.

Except that when we go into the living room Gran is fast asleep. Cosmo says we should wake her up or the Trimmer will scare her but I say it is fine as Gran will sleep through anything, even an earthquake according to Mom, which is true because when I accidentally blew up the oven everyone came running downstairs and Daisy was crying in case it was terrorists, but Gran did not move even a muscle. Plus the Silent Trimmer is not noisy or we will get our money back, according to Aunt Deedee's ad.

And Cosmo is amazed because Gran really does not wake up even when she is bald and looks like her friend Arthur Peason. And we are all totally pleased except that then I remember that I have only done one haircut, which is not enough to pay Mom back for the India phone call and we need to find someone else. So we are racking our brains trying to think of people, but all we can think of is Me, except I do not have any money.

And then I notice that Georgia May Morton-Jones is not racking her brain at all, she is not even in the living room. And then I am worried that a **CATASTROPHE** has happened, i.e. she has been kidnapped by international gangsters. But Cosmo says that **STATISTICALLY** you are more likely to be killed by a donkey than get kidnapped by international gangsters. And he is half right because she has not been kidnapped or killed by a donkey, she is in the kitchen and so is the

Silent Trimmer and she has silently trimmed her head and is now as bald as Gran and Arthur Peason.

Cosmo says that it is actually great news because now Aunt Deedee can give me $15 and I will have made my fortune, but I am not entirely and completely sure because Aunt Deedee is always droning on about how Georgia May Morton-Jones's hair is the envy of The Greely Academy for Girls because of how it is so curly.

And then Georgia May Morton-Jones starts to cry because Barry is chewing the hair on the floor. So then I have my last

BRILLIANT IDEA™,

which is to glue the hair back on to Georgia May Morton-Jones's head.

Only when we have finished, Georgia May Morton-Jones's head does not look like it did before the Silent Trimmer. It is quite a lot of different lengths and there is a big bare spot on the top where we ran out of hair because Barry ate some, plus some more blew into the backyard. And Georgia May starts to cry again and that is when Gran wakes up and Daisy comes downstairs and Mom and Dad come home

all at once which Cosmo says is a **CONSPIRACY**, but it is not, it is a **COINCIDENCE**, and they are not the same – I have checked with Mr. Schumann.

Anyway, a lot of things happen then, which are:

1. Mom turns slightly pale.

b. Gran sees herself in the mirror and thinks all her hair has fallen out like Arthur Peason's and Dad has to sit her in front of Chuck Hernandez, soap opera superstar, for half an hour to calm her down.

3. Barry does a choky noise because he has gotten some of Georgia May's hair stuck in his throat so Dad has to pull it out like on *Animal SOS* and so Barry **MIRACULOUSLY DOES NOT DIE.**

Then Mom says, "Oh merciful heavens, what are we going to tell Aunt Deedee?" And I say, "Well you can tell her it **WASN'T** me, because I only did the gluing part." And Dad calls me Penny Dreadful and does the honking goose laugh and Mom turns even paler and says, "If you cannot say something helpful, Gordon, then don't say anything at all." Then Cosmo says, "I have something helpful to say, i.e. we can glue a hat on the hair so Aunt Deedee won't see the bald spot." And Dad says that is not a bad idea but Mom is not so sure and tells Cosmo it is high time he went home.

But then Mom doesn't have any better ideas so she finds my old policeman's helmet to put on Georgia May Morton-Jones, only Georgia May has been lying on the floor sobbing and has superglued her head to the carpet. So Cosmo says it is either the hair or the carpet that must be chopped off and sacrificed. Mom says, "*I thought I told you to go home, Cosmo Moon Webster.*" But in the end she decides to sacrifice the hair after all, so she gets the Silent Trimmer and shaves Georgia May **AGAIN**.

And that is when
Aunt Deedee walks in.

At first Aunt Deedee **DOES NOT SAY A WORD**.

Which is when Dad has a

BRILLIANT IDEA™,

i.e. to get the vacuum to suck up the clippings, so me and Cosmo and Daisy and Gran all whiz out with him in case it is very heavy and also because of him being not very good with machinery. And then we do not have to listen to Aunt Deedee shouting, which is mostly about how Georgia May will not be allowed to be a princess in The Greely Academy for Girls Ballet Recital because they all have to have regulation buns and she will have to be a bee and wear a furry helmet like Phoebe Patterson-Parry, who everyone knows has two left feet.

Which Cosmo said would be a brilliant way to
make money, having two left feet, because you
would be a phenomenon and people would pay
to look at them. And Dad
says, "Did I ever
tell you I
could have
been a
ballet
dancer if
I hadn't
met your
mother?"
And then
he does a
pirouette

and knocks over a bottle of Grape Soda, which is when Cosmo decides it is time to go home after all.

And I am now doubly gloomy because no one paid me for the haircuts, not even Gran because she says no one will sit next to her at bingo except Arthur Peason. Plus Mom says now I owe Dad $45.99 because the Silent Trimmer is not at all silent any more and it cannot trim either, mainly because it is clogged with superglue.

And Aunt Deedee says no, Dad cannot get his money back because it is **USER ERROR**. So I am not allowed to go to Monkey Madness safari park tomorrow after all.

Daisy says, "*It is all your own fault, Penelope Jones, you are such a complete* **MORON**." But it is not my fault. I am just a

Magnet for Disaster.

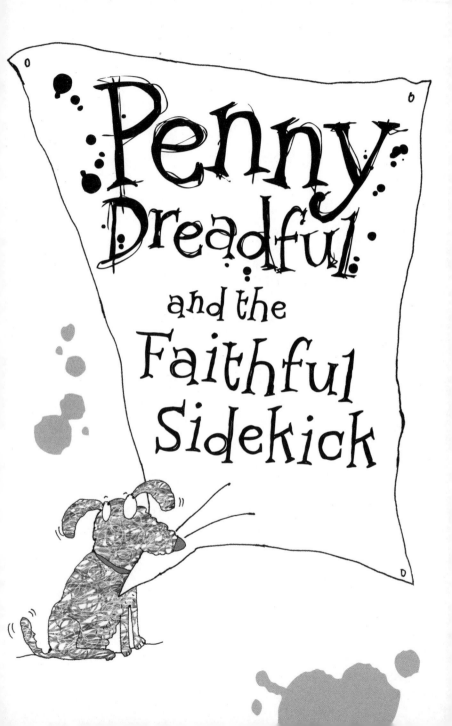

The dog was not
my fault **AT ALL**.

In fact if it is anyone's fault it

is Gran's because she

watches too much

Animal SOS, which

is a TV series

where animals

are always

almost dying but

then they don't and it is

MIRACULOUS, which is

where me and Cosmo got

the idea in the first place.

★ ★ ★ ★

What happened was, we were watching this
episode where they found this huge and hairy
Alsatian which was **COMPLETELY** abandoned
and thin and very sad, and also had a cut
on its paw. And after it **MIRACULOUSLY DID**

NOT DIE a policeman
took it home and
named it Alan and
trained it to be
his faithful
sidekick and
sniff out
burglars
and bad guys.

And then I had my first

BRILLIANT IDEA™,

which was to
have our own
faithful sidekick
because then
we could train
it to sniff out 
criminals or treasure
or at least the chocolate
cookie that I lost last
Wednesday and which

MYSTERIOUSLY

DISAPPEARED very

near Gran's cat Barry.

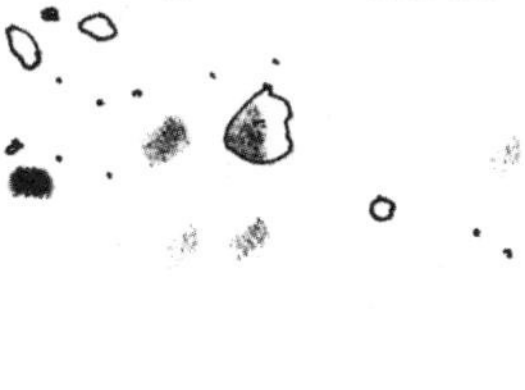

Sniff Sniff

Except that Mom says the only mystery is that Barry is not completely huge and having to be wheeled around on a cart what with all the cereal and cookies and other **NOT CAT FOOD** things that he eats. So then I asked Mom if we could get an Alsatian, only not named Alan, but named Killer or Rex, but she said Alsatians are pedigree dogs and cost hundreds of dollars and I still owe her for the India phone call and the Silent Trimmer thing so no I cannot have one. And Cosmo can't have one because his mom Sunflower is a cat person. Although they do not have a cat either in case the cat kills other animals, which Sunflower is very much against, especially when they are on the kitchen floor in pieces.

So then we are totally **DISCOMBOBULATED**, which is a long word in our spelling bee this week and means **CONFUSED**, according to Miss Patterson our teacher, who is very tall and thin like a beanpole and who said, e.g., "Penelope Jones, I am completely **DISCOMBOBULATED** as to why you have spelled 'Orangutan' with a Q." Only it wasn't a "Q"

it was an "O," but my pen slipped because
Henry Potts threw an eraser at Cosmo but it
hit me by mistake.

But then Gran said in fact cats are very
good sidekicks, e.g. Barry, e.g. he does not like
the man who does the news who looks a little
strange and prefers the nice weather lady with
the long hair so obviously he is a good judge
of character. So I said we could train Barry
just like Alan if we tied a leash onto his collar,
only we didn't have a leash so we used Cosmo's
belt which possibly would have been excellent
except for:

a) Barry did not very much want to be on a
leash and bit my hand and it is **MIRACULOUS**
I did not die because his teeth are very pointy.

b) The only thing Barry could sniff out were cornflakes and he got mad when we did not let him have any because Mom says it is

CAT FOOD AND CAT FOOD ONLY, and so he went back to watching a soap opera on TV with Gran.

3. Cosmo's pants kept falling down
and he tripped over Dad's binoculars
(which I had borrowed to see if
I could look into Mrs. Nugent
across-the-street's living room
because Gran wants to
know if she really does
have a plasma TV
or if it is a lie) and
bumped his head
on the table, which
wobbled and a glass
of orange juice
fell off and landed
on Barry, who is very
hairy and hard to clean.

So then, **d)** Mom said,

> I have had quite enough hoo-hah today what with Daisy and Lucy B. Finnegan who are upstairs trying to be rock stars, and can you please go outside and leave me in peace for five minutes, thank you.

So we did.

★ ☆ ✦ ✦

So in fact it might be Mom's fault, because
if she hadn't made us go out, we would never
have found Rex in the first place.

What happened was that we decided to go
to the general store because there is a quarter
stuck to the sidewalk outside and it is really
fun to watch people try to pick it up, only
when we got to the store the quarter was gone
and a dog was there instead, only not stuck
to the sidewalk, just sitting
on it eating a stick.

And I said,

That dog is thinnish and sad and is possibly **ABANDONED** and we should rescue him and train him to be our faithful sidekick, because if we don't he will have to have a lethal injection and he won't even get to heaven because I have checked and Mr. Schumann said dogs do not get in.

And Cosmo said, "I have seen that dog before, I am not sure he is completely abandoned and maybe we should ask Mrs. Butterworth," who is the lady who works at the general store and has a mustache and who I am not very fond of because she is always saying stuff like "I have got my beady eye on you," and it is very beady, but Cosmo said we had to. Only when we went in Mrs. Butterworth said, "Cosmo Moon Webster and Penelope Jones, go outside immediately — it says **ONLY TWO ST. REGINA'S STUDENTS ALLOWED**, can you not read?" And I said, "Yes we can read but we cannot see through walls and so we did not know that Cherry Scarpelli and Bridget Grimes

were already in here buying chips, which
in fact are bad for you and you might
get clogged and die and end up in heaven
but your dog won't." And Mrs. Butterworth
said she would be reporting
me to my mom for
talking back, so
you see you
cannot win
with her and
her beady eye.

And then
when we got
outside the dog
stood up and
started jumping

up and down a lot so I said it must definitely be abandoned and is trying to tell us to take it home and train it to catch criminals. And Cosmo said, "It is not an Alsatian, it is very small and maybe it is not the right kind of dog." But I said, "It is probably just a puppy and look he has just sniffed that I have some spilled yogurt on my pants so he is obviously **SUPERIORLY INTELLIGENT.**"

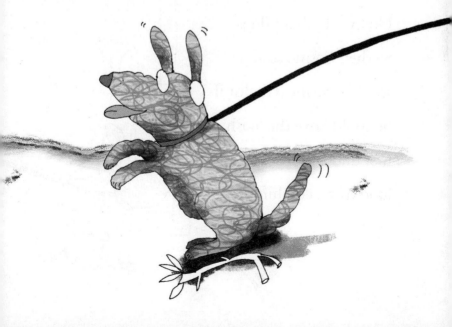

Which is what the policeman
said Alan was. So then Cosmo
said, "Fine but I get to
have the leash because
I am older and a dog
person." And I said no
because I have a Dogs of
the World poster and have
watched *One Hundred
and One Dalmatians* so
I know all about dogs.
So then Cosmo said he
would give me a dollar if
he could have the leash
first and I said yes as
long as we call him Rex.

And Rex was very happy with this arrangement
because he did not bite us or dig his claws in like
Barry, he just walked happily next to Cosmo
and tried to eat lots of stuff like candy
wrappers and a lamp post.

And I said Mom would be very pleased because we had saved her hundreds of dollars in Alsatian money and Dad would be very pleased because he is always saying how he could have been a police dog handler if he hadn't met Mom.

Only when we got home Mom did not seem very pleased at all, in fact her voice went all squeaky and high like it does sometimes and Dad says only dogs and dolphins can understand it. Only Rex did not seem to understand it when she said, "Penelope Jones, what the blazes have you done this time? You get that dog out of here this instant and take it right back where it came from," because he just went on chewing one of

Dad's shoes. And I said, "I can't take him back because he is **COMPLETELY ABANDONED** and they will give him a lethal

injection and he won't even get into heaven," and Gran said, "It is true they do not let dogs into heaven — Arthur Peason was dead for one whole minute when he had his operation and the man at the gates told him his spaniel Maurice couldn't come in and that is the only reason Arthur is alive today."

And Mom said, "I do not have time for this, I have to be at the office in five minutes but I do not want to see that dog when I get home." And I said she wouldn't, he would be **MIRACULOUSLY ELSEWHERE**, i.e. at Cosmo's possibly.

Only when she had gone Cosmo reminded me that Sunflower is a cat person and that she is not big on dogs because they are not very intelligent and have a bad aura. And I said Rex was in fact **SUPERIORLY INTELLIGENT** except he wasn't showing it at that exact moment because he was too busy trying to get into the washing machine, unless he was trying to say he needed a bath in which case he was doubly clever.

But Cosmo still said no and so did Lucy B.
Finnegan because she already has a parakeet
and gerbils, and Daisy said,

You are a **MORON** if you think
anyone is going to want that
hairy thing, Penelope Jones.

And then they went back upstairs
to be rock stars again.

So that is when I had my

BRILLIANT IDEA™

number two, which was that Aunt Deedee

is a dog person and she had to send her dog

Llewellyn back to the pet store because he kept

nipping at Georgia May Morton-Jones (i.e. my

cousin) and her fingers are very important

because Mr. Nakamura says she shows

potential on the violin. And I said Rex

is not at all nippy and he is just the kind of

dog that Aunt Deedee might like and it will

make her less mad at me after the Silent

Trimmer thing so it is definitely a

BRILLIANT IDEA™

★ ☆ ✦ ✦

So me and Cosmo took Rex over to Aunt
Deedee's house, which is only four streets away
but it is very much bigger than ours and also
much cleaner because of all the rules, e.g.:

1. No eating except at the table.

2. No clay or paint or glue except at
the table and only if it is covered in a
plastic cloth.

C. No eating clay or paint or glue.

Plus if you even **LOOK** at a glass
candlestick she says, "Do not even think
about it, Penelope Jones." Only when we
got there Aunt Deedee was at work, i.e. on a

CONFERENCE CALL WITH THE NEW YORK OFFICE, and Georgia May Morton-Jones was being taken care of by the new nanny who is named Lilya Bobylev and is from Russia (which is where all nannies come from) and has not been fired yet for **NOT MEASURING UP** although Gran says it is only a matter of time.

So I said,

Hello, Lilya Bobylev, this is Rex, he is for Aunt Deedee. She definitely wants him because he is not nippy and will not eat Georgia May's fingers so she can play violin.

And Lilya said,

I do not think Mrs. Morton-Jones very happy with dog.

And I said,

Yes she is, she is a dog person and you have to keep him because of the hair shaving.

And then there was a crash from the dining room because Georgia May had accidentally poked a glass candlestick with her violin bow, so Lilya had to go and glue it back together (but only at the table with the cloth), so we just went in.

Georgia May did not seem very pleased with Rex either at first because of her violin fingers, but then Cosmo showed her he is not at all nippy and then he put his head in Rex's mouth like a lion, only he did not leave it there long because he said it smelled like meat and he is vegetarian.

So then Georgia May seemed a little happier
and said we could dress Rex up in her tutu and
her furry bee hat (that she had to wear for
ballet because of not having a regulation bun)
because he would be much prettier that way.

And she was right, Rex did look much
prettier in a tutu and a bee helmet, only
he did not want to dance to her Children's
Introduction to
Mozart CD,

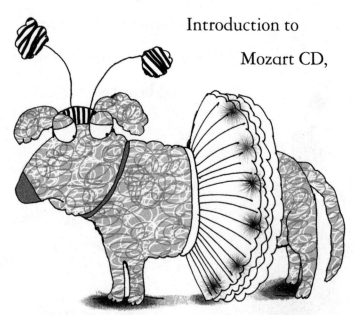

he wanted to swallow things. In fact quite a
lot of things, i.e.:

1. Four chocolate cookies

b. A banana

c) The key to the back door

4. And the receiver of

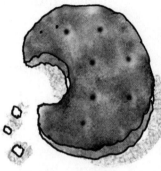

Georgia May Morton-Jones's
baby monitor, which Aunt Deedee
still uses because she can make
sure Georgia May is practicing
her violin and also issue
instructions to Lilya.

★ ☆ ✦ ✷

Lilya said, "This not good at all,
Mrs. Morton-Jones not happy,"
and Cosmo said, "She *is* never happy,

so eating the key and the monitor won't make much difference." Which is true. But Lilya did not agree and said we had to take the bee helmet and tutu off Rex and then go home and Georgia May had to go to her room and do Mandarin practice (which is not about being an orange, it is another language, like Chinese). So Georgia May went upstairs and then an amazing thing happened because suddenly we could hear her saying *"Wo Jiao Georgia May Morton-Jones,"* only it did not come out of her mouth it came right out of Rex. And Cosmo said, "It is the other end of the baby monitor." And he went upstairs and got the speaker part and showed us by saying

I am Rex the all-powerful and if you do not do as I say I will put you on my sacrificial altar

in his Darth Vadar voice
(because he is really in to
Darth Vadar
and sacrificial altars)
and it was fantastic
because the voice
came right
out of Rex.

Although I am not sure that Rex thought it was fantastic – in fact he looked completely **DISCOMBOBULATED**. But anyway then I had a try and I made Rex sound like Mrs. Butterworth by saying "*I have my beady eye on you*" a lot. And then even Lilya wanted to do it and she made Rex sing a Russian song, which was doubly **DISCOMBOBULATING** and not just for Rex. And that is when Aunt Deedee walked in.

At first Aunt Deedee was also **DISCOMBOBULATED** because there was a dog singing in Russian in her living room dressed in a tutu and a furry bee helmet, but then she saw me and Cosmo and she said a lot of things starting with how I am a

complete and utter
nuisance and which ended
up with her firing Lilya
and calling Mom.

★ ★ ★ ★

Mom was not at all happy about coming because
she had only just gotten home from work and
Daisy was crying because Lucy B. Finnegan said
she was not at all in tune, so Mom made Dad
come too, who was also not happy about coming
because Barry had rubbed against his leg and it
was all sticky from the spilled juice.

When they got here Aunt Deedee showed
them the baby monitor thing by
talking
into it
and saying,

I have had
it up to here
with your
daughter,
she is a **BAD
INFLUENCE**.
This cost
$149.99.

Only of course Rex said it, which was actually

very scary.

And Cosmo said, "It will be okay because
Rex will just poop it out in a day or so
and then you can have it back," but Aunt
Deedee did not want the monitor back and Rex
said so. And then Mom said, "I told you I
wanted that dog out of my sight," and
I said, "He was out of your sight only you
came over here, so it is not my fault,
it is yours," and Dad said, "Penny Dreadful!"
and did the honking goose laugh, only Mom
gave him one of her looks so he turned it into
a cough and said,

Where did you get the
dog from anyway?

And Cosmo said outside the general store, and I said how Rex was completely **ABANDONED** and about to have a lethal injection and not get into heaven, etc., but Dad said, "No he wasn't, he has a tag on his collar, look." And we did look and he was right and the tag said,

My name is
Clarence
– if I am lost
please return me
to Mrs. Higgins
at 19 Newton
Street

And Cosmo said, "Oh that is where I have seen him before," because Cosmo lives at 21 Newton Street, i.e. next door, and Mom gave Cosmo one of her looks and he decided it was time to go home. And I said Clarence was not a good name for a faithful sidekick, he should be Rex or Killer, and Mom gave me one of her looks so I decided it was time to go home too. Only Dad said I couldn't, I had to go with him to take Clarence back to Mrs. Higgins, so in the end me and Cosmo both went while Mom paid for the baby monitor and tried to get Lilya unfired.

★ ☆ ✦ ✸

Mrs. Higgins was completely happy to see Clarence and said she had only left him outside the general store while she went in for some eggs and when she came out he had **VANISHED INTO THIN AIR** and where on earth did we find him?

Dad said he was on Hollyhock Road, which is not a complete lie because that is where Aunt Deedee lives and anyway it is for the **GREATER GOOD**.

And Mrs. Higgins said, "Oh thank you, I was so worried because he is on a special diet and if you are not careful he will eat anything. He has not eaten anything, has he?" And Dad said no, which was another lie but was also for the **GREATER GOOD**, or at least he says it will be as long as Rex does not go near Aunt Deedee's house and the other end of the baby monitor for a while, because that could be quite shocking for Mrs. Higgins.

★ ☆ ★ ✦

So now we are not allowed **EVER** to get a faithful sidekick because Mom says I have proved I am **NOT RESPONSIBLE** with animals, plus now I owe her for the baby monitor as well and will be paying her back **UNTIL KINGDOM COME**, so I asked her when Kingdom would come but she gave me another one of her looks, so I shut up then.

Daisy said, "*It is all your own fault, Penelope Jones, you are such a complete* **MORON**." But it is not my fault. I am just a

Magnet
for
Disaster.

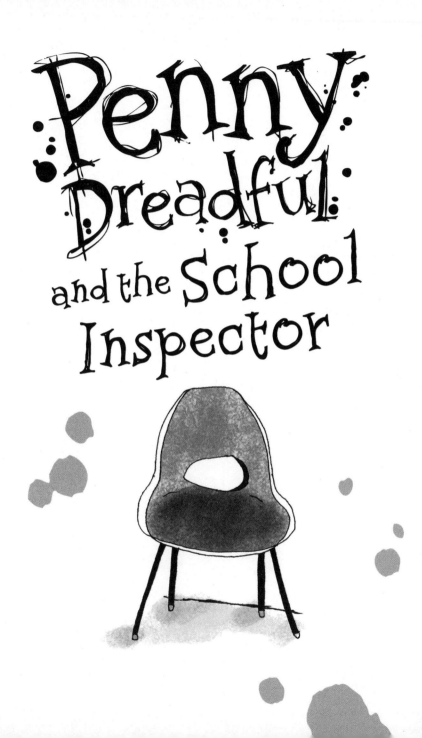

Mr. Schumann is our principal

and he mostly says things like "Penelope Jones, I am **SICK AND TIRED** of seeing you on the naughty chair," which is not actually a chair that has been naughty, it is a chair for naughty people which is outside his office, and it is true I am quite often on it even though I am not actually naughty, I am just a **MAGNET FOR DISASTER**.

Anyway he has been **SICK AND TIRED** even more than usual because a School Inspector is coming to St. Regina's to make sure that it is **UP TO SCRATCH**,

otherwise it will be shut down and we will all have to be bussed to Chipping Broadley Elementary School, which I said sounded actually quite wonderful but Bridget Grimes (who is the star student and Mr. Schumann's favorite) said her mother said Mrs. Butterworth in the general store said that the Burton twins go there and they have ringworm and drink ketchup, plus the bus smells disgusting ever since the trip to Mole Hall Wildlife Park, so we are better off at St. Regina's. Although I have seen Cosmo drink ketchup and he has had lice three times this year, so it is just the smelly bus really.

So on Thursday Mr. Schumann comes into our classroom at circle time (which is when we are supposed to be all sitting on the floor talking about history and other interesting things, except that I am in the corner with Cosmo because we have had an argument with Bridget Grimes about otters) and he tells Miss Patterson (who is our teacher and who is very tall and thin like a beanpole) that we have to be on our best behavior and there is to be absolutely **NO NONSENSE OR SHENANIGANS** whatsoever and if there is then whoever does the shenanigans will be in **BIG TROUBLE**. And when he says that he looks me right in the eye, which is not completely fair because I have only been in **BIG TROUBLE** four times this semester:

1. For sticking a gel pen up Bridget Grimes's nose to see if it would reach her brain, which it did not, but it is not because she does not have one, which is what  Cosmo said, it is because noses are not made for pens, according to Miss Patterson.

2. For bringing Barry to school in my bag for show-and-tell, although in fact he was the most interesting show-and-tell **EVER** because

he ran up the curtain in the cafeteria and got stuck and the fire department

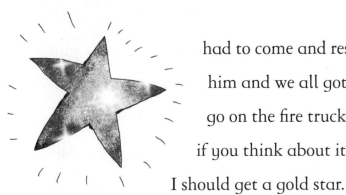

had to come and rescue
him and we all got to
go on the fire truck, so
if you think about it
I should get a gold star.

C. For telling Mr. Schumann that Gran was
dead and that I would not be able to do my
math homework because I had to sit by her
grave and weep.

4. For proving that the most cookies you
can eat before you are sick is twenty-three
which is actually quite scientific
so in fact I should get another
gold star.

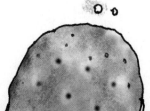

Anyway, then he says the Inspector is coming at nine o'clock tomorrow so we have twenty-four hours to **SHARPEN UP OUR ACT**, which means absolutely no throwing erasers at people and absolutely lots of math. Cosmo says actually it is only nineteen hours because it is two o'clock already and maybe Mr. Schumann should absolutely do lots of math too, but Mr. Schumann does not look like he wants to do math, he looks like he wants to throw an eraser at Cosmo but luckily he can't because that would be **SHENANIGANS**.

Mr. Schumann also says it is **STRICTLY UNIFORM ONLY** tomorrow, i.e. red top, gray bottoms, white socks and black shoes, and he looks at me again at that part, because I am not

wearing a red top I am wearing a green one
(which is not entirely my fault, it is because
I was showing Daisy how it is possible to drink
Sugar Pops out of the bowl upside down, only it
turns out it is not possible and they just fall all
over you), and also at Cosmo, because Cosmo
is wearing a Jedi outfit and rain boots.

★ ★ ★ ★

So the next morning I make sure I am almost
completely wearing **STRICTLY UNIFORM ONLY**,
i.e. my red top because Mom
has gotten most of the
Sugar Pops out with a
sponge, and it is only
my socks which are
not **STRICT** because
yesterday's white ones
have holes in them from
where I showed
Cosmo how to
make a glove
puppet and the only
ones left are striped ones,

but at least it is red and white stripes so it is half **STRICT**.

But when I meet Cosmo at the end of Newton Street he is **NOT IN UNIFORM AT ALL**. This is because Sunflower, his mom, who is actually named Barbara, does not believe in uniforms because they rae oppressive and made of polyester; she believes in **FREEDOM** and **SELF-EXPRESSION** and also in natural fibers, so Cosmo is wearing a long cloak and flip-flops.

I say Mr. Schumann will not be happy, in fact he will be **SICK AND TIRED**, but Cosmo says he has an official letter from Sunflower saying it is against the law to make him wear a uniform until he is eleven and she will stage a one-woman sit-in protest outside Mr. Schumann's office if he tries to send Cosmo home.

Which is exactly what Mr. Schumann tries to do when Cosmo walks into school, only Cosmo shows him the official letter and

Mr. Schumann decides he does not want
Sunflower sitting outside his office protesting
when the School Inspector is here,

so he says Cosmo will just have
to say it is religious grounds.
Then he tells Miss Patterson
to put me and Cosmo at the back
of class where we are almost hidden by
Alexander Pringle, who wears age-14 size clothes
even though he is nine because of his glands
and also because he is always eating, and so
the School Inspector
will possibly not
see that Cosmo
is wearing
the cloak.

But when Mr. Schumann has gone back to his office to wait, Bridget Grimes puts her hand up and says,

But Miss Patterson, if they are at the back then they will whisper and throw things which is **SHENANIGANS**.

Miss Patterson decides that Bridget Grimes is
right and she makes us trade with Luke Bruce
and Brady O'Grady, who are more in the middle.
Only then Cosmo is utterly visible and plus also

he is right next to Henry Potts who is his mortal enemy, and almost immediately Cosmo has to throw an eraser at him and it misses and hits a jar of blue paint, which spills all over Bridget Grimes's gray bottoms so she has to get changed into her PE shorts,

which are not gray
at all but are purple
and have butterflies
on them. So then Miss
Patterson decides we should

go back to where Mr. Schumann put us,
so we have to trade again with Luke Bruce
and Brady O'Grady and sit next to the locust
tank, which is good because you can watch
them scuttling around and jumping like
grasshoppers through the special shatterproof
glass. Except that Miss Patterson says there is
to be absolutely no staring at the locusts and
instead we have to stare at the whiteboard
and concentrate on the lots of math because the
School Inspector will be here **ANY MINUTE**.

But he is not here **ANY MINUTE** because after about a whole hour I notice out of the corner of my eye (which is mostly staring at the whiteboard) that Mr. Schumann is standing at the gate looking up and down the street and he is almost definitely **SICK AND TIRED**. And by this point everyone is getting a little

SICK AND TIRED of all the math and even Bridget Grimes has gotten two answers wrong, which is a **MIRACLE** and so she is crying

and Luke Bruce
is asleep

and Alexander
Pringle is eating
a jelly sandwich.

So Miss Patterson decides that we have possibly done enough math even for Mr. Schumann and that maybe we should do some art instead because it is important to show that we are creative as well as knowing how many nines make forty-five, but that we cannot use the paint as there has already been one accident so we will do collages instead.

And so we get the scissors and glue and cardboard and glitter out and me and Cosmo decide we are going to do a collage of aliens invading Planet Earth, and then everyone is cutting and gluing like **CRAZY**, only then Cosmo notices that

he has accidentally glued his cloak to the desk
and so Miss Patterson makes him take it off
and underneath is the Jedi outfit, and I can tell
Miss Patterson is
beginning to
be **SICK**

AND

TIRED

too.

Especially because then Brady O'Grady pours all the glitter over his head because he says he is part of his own collage, which under normal circumstances Miss Patterson would say is actually quite **CREATIVE** but today she just says, "I think that is quite enough art for today and maybe we should do our topic of Ancient Egypt because they did not have glue or glitter there."

We are going to try to build pyramids out of the wooden blocks like Egyptian slaves, which is math and creativity at once, and Mr. Schumann will be totally **NOT SICK AND TIRED**. And Miss Patterson says me and Cosmo can work with Bridget Grimes and Cherry Scarpelli because they will cancel us out with their brains. But actually she is wrong because it turns out that me and Cosmo are totally exceptional at pyramids and we build our side super-fast

and Bridget Grimes gets mad and says,
"Miss Patterson, Penelope Jones and
Cosmo Moon Webster have hogged all
the blocks and I don't have a single one."
So then Henry Potts throws a block
at Bridget Grimes but it misses

and hits me on the nose.

So I throw it back at Henry only it misses him and hits the locust tank, which it turns out is not shatterproof after all and it breaks and all the locusts fly out.

And that is when Mr. Schumann and the School Inspector walk in.

And everyone goes very quiet, except
Bridget Grimes, who is crying because there
are several locusts stuck in her hair,

and also the locusts are not completely quiet,
they are really buzzy. And Mr. Schumann is
looking right at me, even though he cannot
know it is me who threw the block at the

locust tank unless he has X-ray eyes, which are
not real they are only in movies, so I say,

Actually it is totally on purpose, Mr. Schumann, because we are being Ancient Egyptians and there were a lot of locusts in Ancient Egypt.

And Cosmo says,

Yes there was a complete plague of them and they devoured everything in their path.

Then Bridget Grimes cries even more because
she says the locusts are going to devour her.
Only Alexander Pringle says if she does not be
quiet *he* will devour her and he once ate four
servings of banana pudding at lunch so Bridget
shuts up quickly. And then Miss Patterson
decides it is time we did PE and so she sends
everyone out to change into their shorts, except
Bridget who is already in hers, and Cosmo, who
says he has an official letter not to do PE because
it is too **COMPETITIVE AND AGGRESSIVE**,
and me, because she says I have to go and sit on
the naughty chair and wait for Mr. Schumann
to punish me. And the whole time Mr. Schumann
is looking completely **SICK AND TIRED** and the
Inspector is writing like **CRAZY** in his notebook

and I think he is definitely writing down that

St. Regina's has to be closed because of the

NOT AT ALL STRICT UNIFORM and the

fighting and the escaped locusts

(which have noticed the door and are all heading out

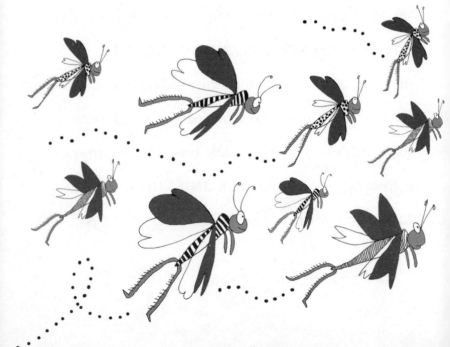

of it in a giant swarm).

And then it gets worse when I am sitting on the chair, because the School Inspector comes and sits on another not-naughty chair next to me and asks me a lot of questions about the chair, i.e. *how many times have you had to sit on the naughty chair? What kinds of things have you been sent to sit on the chair for? How many lessons have you missed to sit on the chair?* And Mr. Schumann is standing behind him staring me right in the eye, so I absolutely **DO NOT LIE** and I say I have sat on it at least twenty-seven times this year, mostly for throwing stuff,

and I have missed math several times and
the trip to the museum to see the stuffed lion
and the Roman coins.

And I am thinking that even if St. Regina's is not closed down then I am going to be in **BIG TROUBLE** again and possibly even excluded forever.

And when I get home I have to tell Mom and Dad what has happened and Daisy says,

It is all your own fault, Penelope Jones, you are such a **MORON**!

even though it is **OBVIOUS** that it is Henry Potts's fault because he threw the block first,

or possibly Bridget's fault for saying she didn't
have a block. And anyway Daisy should
be sad because now I am going to
be shipped off on the bus to
Chipping Broadley Elementary
School with the Burton Twins and
probably get ringworm and have
to drink ketchup. Only Daisy
says in fact I can be
home-schooled like
Fraser Forks, who gets to make peach
cobbler and read about whales all day and it is
unfair and why can't we both be home-schooled?
And Mom says **NO ONE** is being home-schooled
because she would rather try to teach Barry to
knit, and to please stop all the nonsense.

✶ ✫ ✷ ✹

Only a very **UNUSUAL** thing happens when I
go into school on Monday. Which is that the
school is not shut down and I am not sent to
Chipping Broadley Elementary School to drink
ketchup and catch ringworm, or home to make
peach cobbler and read about whales. But there
is a very big change, apart from the locusts,
which Miss Patterson says were last seen
heading toward Chipping Broadley,

and that is that the

naughty chair

has completely

VANISHED

And when I ask Mr. Schumann where it is he says it is in the closet because apparently it is not very **PROGRESSIVE** to have a naughty chair and miss trips to museums. So in fact it is entirely my fault.

And for once I do not argue.

Penny Dreadful's Top 5 Tips for Survival

Sometimes it is very **ARDUOUS** being a **MAGNET FOR DISASTER**. Especially if you are extra specially magnetic, i.e. like me. But even though it is **ARDUOUS**, it is also very **INFORMATIVE**, i.e. I have learned some important **TOP TIPS** about how to avoid complete **CATASTROPHE**.

Number 1

Get a DISGUISE

It is completely

important not to

look like me, i.e.

Penelope Jones,

when I am being

very magnetic,

e.g. accidentally

knocking over a teetering stack of bean cans

at the general store. So sometimes I dress up as

Cosmo, i.e. in a Jedi outfit and rain boots,

because it completely confuses Mrs.

Butterworth's beady eye and however hard she

RACKS her brain she is **DISCOMBOBULATED**

as to who to shout at.

Another good disguise is dressing up as a burglar, because burglars wear balaclavas which **COMPLETELY** cover up their face. Although it is possible you would get shouted at for being a burglar anyway.

Number 2
Collect COLLATERAL, i.e. money

Coins are **EVERYWHERE**, e.g. on the ground outside the general store, down the back of the sofa and mostly in Dad's pants pockets.

Collect them **ALL** because you never know

what you might need them for:

1. Paying people back, e.g. your Aunt Deedee

when you have accidentally broken a glass

vase or called Russia for instance.

b) Buying essential supplies

like cookies or licorice sticks.

iii. Playing ludo, because you have

used the actual plastic counters to

flick at your mortal enemy.

Number 3
Be PREPARED for EVERY EVENTUALITY

DISASTERS are EVERYWHERE and you never

know when you might be super-magnetic,

so it is completely important to have a box

of useful things for **EVERY EVENTUALITY,**

i.e. anything, e.g.:

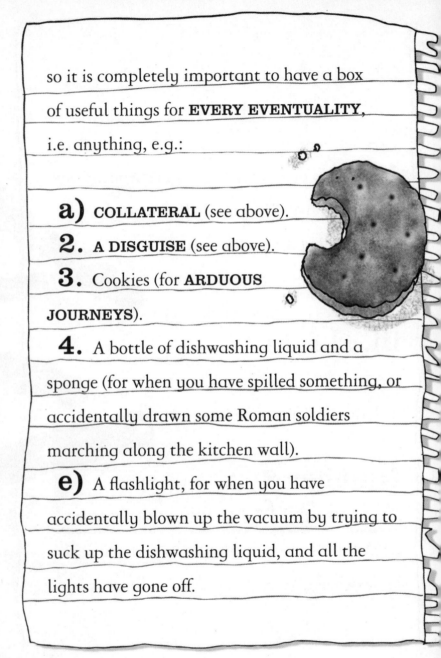

a) **COLLATERAL** (see above).

2. **A DISGUISE** (see above).

3. Cookies (for **ARDUOUS**

JOURNEYS).

4. A bottle of dishwashing liquid and a

sponge (for when you have spilled something, or

accidentally drawn some Roman soldiers

marching along the kitchen wall).

e) A flashlight, for when you have

accidentally blown up the vacuum by trying to

suck up the dishwashing liquid, and all the

lights have gone off.

Number 4

Find a TRUSTY SCAPEGOAT

This means someone else to **BLAME**, e.g. in our house everyone mostly blames me, even though it is not usually my fault, it is that I am a **MAGNET FOR DISASTER**. So I usually blame Barry the cat, because he is most often eating things that are **NOT** cat food. E.g. when Daisy said, "Where is my last chocolate-covered cherry, Penelope Jones? *I* **KNOW** *it is you who has eaten it,*" I said, "But in fact maybe it is not I, it is **BARRY**, because he completely **ADORES** cherries and chocolate, so ha!"

Number 5

Get a FAITHFUL FRIEND

If you are very magnetic like me, it is
COMPLETELY important to have a faithful
friend, which is not the same thing as a
scapegoat, and is also not the same as a dog
(especially not one that isn't yours but which
you have found outside the general store only it
is not lost at all) but e.g. Cosmo Moon Webster.
Because faithful friends will always stand up
for you, even when you have accidentally
exploded pudding in their microwave,
and even if they are a boy
and exactly a week
older than you.

My
Faithful Friend

Joanna Nadin

wrote this book –
and lots of others
like it. She is small,
funny, clever,
sneaky and musical.

Before she became a writer, she wanted to be a
champion ballroom dancer or a jockey, but she
was actually a lifeguard at a swimming pool,
a radio newsreader, a cleaner in an old people's
home, and a juggler. She likes peanut butter on
toast for breakfast, and jam on toast for dessert.
Her perfect day would involve baking, surfing,
sitting in cafes in Paris, and playing with her
daughter – who reminds her a lot of
Penny Dreadful…

Jess Mikhail

illustrated this book. She loves creating funny characters with bright colors and fancy

patterns to make people smile. Her favorite place is her tiny home, where she lives with her tiny dog and spends lots of time drawing, scanning, scribbling, printing, stamping, and sometimes using her scary computer. She loves to rummage through a good charity shop to find weird and wonderful things. A perfect day for her would have to involve a sunny beach and large amounts of spicy foods and ice cream (not together).

For Millie, Katherine and Freddie,
who are all magnets for disaster,
but not at all dreadful.

First published in the UK in 2011 by Usborne Publishing Ltd., Usborne House,
83-85 Saffron Hill, London EC1N 8RT, England. www.usborne.com

A CIP catalogue record for this book is available from the British Library.

First published in America in 2014 AE.

PB ISBN 9780794523251
ALB ISBN 9781601303417
JFMAMJJA OND/14 02349/11
Printed in Dongguan, Guangdong, China.

Maris
J
Purpledot